Clap Clap!

Clap Clap!

BY

Mary Claire Helldorfer

ILLUSTRATED BY

Sandra Speidel

VIKING

Clap clap!
The Lord unrolls the day.

Laugh—
he splashes water
over sunny rocks.

Sing high,
sing low.
Run up
and down
his rippling
hills.

Hoot!

He blows gold lilies

into trumpets.

Hush now.

The Lord hears

we are sorry.

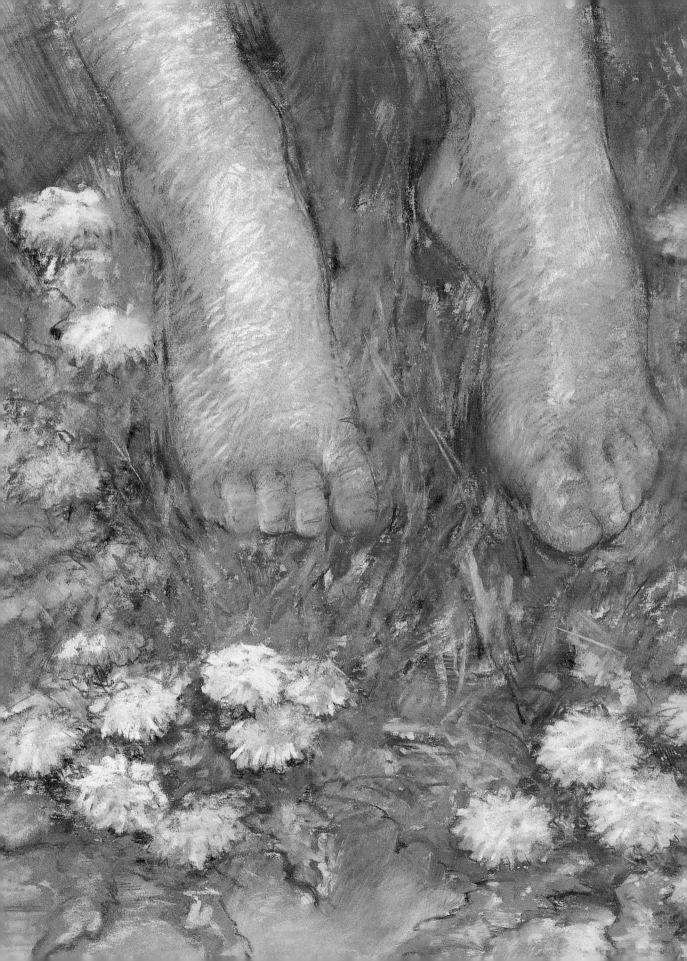

Dance—

he gave us springy heels and toes.

Spin,
then stop and feel
his earth turning beneath
our feet.

Stretch
to find the height
he has hidden within us.

Chase—
he draws us on
with dandelion feathers
and fireflies.

Touch
candle to candle.
He changes air
to petals of light.

Cry.

He made arms to hold.

Hold some more.

Count
the stars he hangs:
see how far hope
shines.

Sleep now.
Now peace.
His moon roosts
in a tree.

Up! Up!
The Lord is waiting
to show us what
he just made.

For Uncle Dick,

who made us laugh and sing,

and Aunt Mary Lee,

a petal of light

—M.C.H.

To my daughter Zoe Speidel,

Alana McDonald,

and Greggy Johnson

—S.S.

VIKING
Published by the Penguin Group
Penguin Books USA Inc., 375 Hudson Street, New York, New York 10014, U.S.A.
Penguin Books Ltd, 27 Wrights Lane, London W8 5TZ, England
Penguin Books Australia Ltd, Ringwood, Victoria, Australia
Penguin Books Canada Ltd, 10 Alcorn Avenue, Toronto, Ontario, Canada M4V 3B2
Penguin Books (N.Z.) Ltd, 182–190 Wairau Road, Auckland 10, New Zealand

Penguin Books Ltd, Registered Offices: Harmondsworth, Middlesex, England

First published in 1993 by Viking, a division of Penguin Books USA Inc.

1 3 5 7 9 10 8 6 4 2

Text copyright © Mary Claire Helldorfer, 1993
Illustrations copyright © Sandra Speidel, 1993
All rights reserved

Library of Congress Cataloging-in-Publication Data
Helldorfer, Mary Claire, 1954–   Clap clap! / Mary Claire Helldorfer ;
illustrated by Sandra Speidel.   p.   cm.
Summary: The reader is exhorted to sing, count, listen,
touch, and dance in celebration of the miracle of each day.
I S B N 0 - 6 7 0 - 8 5 1 5 5 - 8
[1. Conduct of life—Fiction. 2. Christian life—Fiction.]
I. Speidel, Sandra, ill. II. Title.
PZ7.H37418C1 1993 [E]—dc20   93-12585 CIP AC

Printed in Hong Kong   Set in 22 point Galliard Bold